BARK PARK

To dog-lovers everywhere,
but especially to Doug, Julie, and Alex.
Thanks, Julie, for the title!
And with all my love to Nina and Lee,
even though they prefer cats.

—K. G. R

Ω
Published by
PEACHTREE PUBLISHERS
1700 Chattahoochee Avenue
Atlanta, Georgia 30318-2112
www.peachtree-online.com

Text and illustrations © 2008 by Karen Gray Ruelle

First trade paperback edition published in 2013

Art direction by Loraine M. Joyner
Typesetting by Melanie McMahon Ives

The illustrations were created as collages using papers hand-painted in watercolor. Titles are hand-lettered and digitized in Adobe Illustrator. Text is typeset in International Type Corporation's Stone Sans.

Printed in July 2013 by Imago in Singapore
10 9 8 7 6 5 4 3 (hardcover)
10 9 8 7 6 5 4 3 2 1 (trade paperback)

Library of Congress Cataloging-in-Publication Data

Ruelle, Karen Gray.
  Bark park / written and illustrated by Karen Gray Ruelle.— 1st ed.
      p. cm.
  Summary: Illustrations and rhyming text reveal dogs of every shape, size, and personality as they romp and frolic in a park.
  ISBN 13: 978-1-56145-434-1 / ISBN 10: 1-56145-434-6 (hardcover)
  ISBN 13: 978-1-56145-773-1 / ISBN 10: 1-56145-773-6 (trade paperback)
[1. Dogs—Fiction. 2. Parks—Fiction. 3. Stories in rhyme.] I. Title.
  PZ8.3.R86Bar 2007
  [E]—dc22
                          2007029753

BARK PARK

written and illustrated by

Karen Gray Ruelle

PEACHTREE
ATLANTA

Hound dog, round dog, on the run.

Strolling, rolling, having fun.

Small dog, tall dog, down the street.

Dashing, splashing, old friends meet.

Hot dog, dot dog,
in the park.

Fat dog, rat dog.
Bark! Bark! Bark!

Strong dog, long dog,
fetching sticks.

Begging, rolling,
doing tricks.

Thin dog, grin dog,
gulping, lapping.

Hairless, careless, digging, yapping.

Pack dog, track dog,
on the prowl.

Curly, surly,
woof and growl.

Dark dog, bark dog, raising hackles.

Grumpy, jumpy, making tackles.

Sneak dog, leak dog,
owners shout!
Wagging, dragging,
heading out.

Mutt dog, strut dog,
one and all.

Finding toy
and bone and ball.

Old dog, cold dog,
now it's dark.

Guide dog, ride dog,
leave the park.

Roam dog, home dog,
eating snacks.

Bathing, brushing,
rubbing backs.

Lap dog, nap dog,
snuggle up.

Shaggy, waggy,
sleepy pup.

Snow dog, bow dog,
curled up tight.

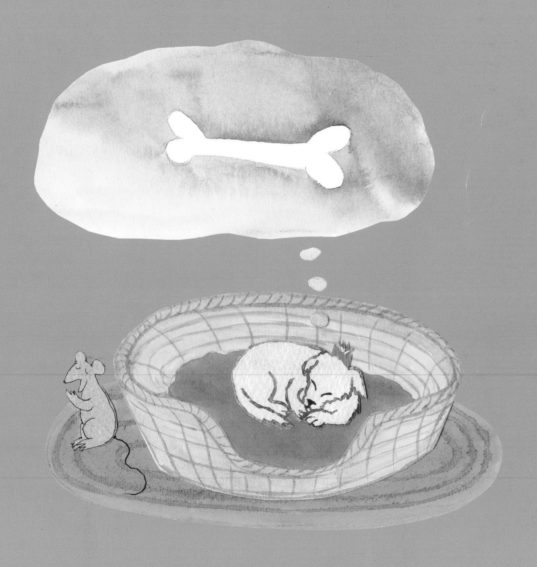

Doggie-dreaming
through the night.

This book grew out of some art I did for an exhibit, "The Dog Days of Summer," during the summer of 1999 at The Enchanted Forest in SoHo, in New York City. I did a series of cut-out dogs, painted with watercolor, as well as some clay dog puppets and handmade books about dogs. One of the pieces was a "Pack of Dogs" which was a small box containing fifty-two different dog cut-outs, as well as two joker dogs.

The text was inspired by many visits to the dog run in New York City's Tompkins Square Park.